T0130401

THE PRINCESS AND THE PINK GIRAFFE

By Christopher Pearson

Inspired by Naimah Pearson

Copyright © 2020 Christopher Pearson.

Illustrated by Amelia Clay

All rights reserved. No part of this book may be used or reproduced by any means, graphic, electronic, or mechanical, including photocopying, recording, taping or by any information storage retrieval system without the written permission of the author except in the case of brief quotations embodied in critical articles and reviews.

Balboa Press books may be ordered through booksellers or by contacting:

Balboa Press
A Division of Hay House
1663 Liberty Drive
Bloomington, IN 47403
www.balboapress.com
844-682-1282

Because of the dynamic nature of the Internet, any web addresses or links contained in this book may have changed since publication and may no longer be valid. The views expressed in this work are solely those of the author and do not necessarily reflect the views of the publisher, and the publisher hereby disclaims any responsibility for them.

Any people depicted in stock imagery provided by Getty Images are models, and such images are being used for illustrative purposes only.
Certain stock imagery © Getty Images.

ISBN: 978-1-9822-5182-6 (sc)
ISBN: 978-1-9822-5183-3 (e)

Print information available on the last page.

Balboa Press rev. date: 08/07/2020

Facebook: Christopher Pearson
Instagram: Christopher Pearson12
Twitter: @christo81547663
Email: Christopherpearson1118@outlook.com

BALBOA.PRESS

Far away in a magical land, there lived a beautiful
princess, and life for her was quite grand.

Birds would chirp melodies angelic and clean, as they sung together on the branches of colorful trees.

Flowers would sway from right to the left, with an aroma
so pleasant, anyone who was fortunate enough to
catch a whiff would surely say it was the best.

The beautiful princess was adored far and wide, with all desiring her attention, hoping greatly to one day be by her side.

She made friends easily, naturally she was kind, smart, she loved learning, and she would always go to bed on time.

In the morning when she would wake up, from such a pleasant sleep, she made sure to wash her face, and always enjoyed brushing her teeth, and never leaving her castle until her room was nice and neat.

On a lovely spring morning, when the sun was radiant and strong, the princess became startled the very moment, a large lion came moseying along.

Greetings gorgeous princess! I hope you are not afraid.
I come in peace, there is one much more remarkable
than I, along your path, if only you travel east.

The lion spoke eloquently, there was not a sign of deception not at all.
The lion looked off into the distance, as he pointed east with his paw.

What could be this wonder, that the lion spoke of,
and encouraged the princess to see?

Could it be a treasure, full of fl awless diamonds, rubies
and gems or could it be a feast of delicious foods, that
the princess can share with all her friends?

There off into the distance, held a figure uncommon and strange.
Taken by surprise, and she wondered if the animal had a name?

The closer the princess came, it was clear and was no lie, that this was indeed a pink giraffe, and alone she surely did cry.

To see a giraffe this hue, was indeed something new, and the fact that she was also sad, the princess did not know what to do.

Excuse me giraffe, do you have a name, and what is wrong? I could not help but notice you are crying, and all alone.

My name is Eema, and there is nothing you can do to help. All the other giraffes won't play with me because I am different, and have left me by myself.

The princess did not like this one bit, and indeed this was a shame.
The princess thought..."Fore what if I were pink,
would my friends treat me the same?"

I will play with you, you can come with me. I will share my toys with you, we will have so much fun, you just wait and see.

The princess lead the way, and the pink giraffe followed closely behind.
Once inside the magical land, the pink giraffe will fi t in just fi ne.

There were trees with pink leaves, where the
singing birds sung their melodies
Children wore shirts with pink sleeves,
everyone getting along in harmony.

The pink giraffe could not believe her eyes, to her surprise, no longer was she sad. She was even making new friends. And for once, things were not as bad.

See Eema I told you, you would like it, and you are invited to stay however long you wish. You are beautiful because you are different, don't allow someone else's ignorance cause you to forget.

The princess and the pink giraffe spent the whole rest of the day dancing and having fun. It is amazing how just a little bit of kindness can really help someone.

Printed in the United States
By Bookmasters